The Good Deed

WRITTEN BY Anna de Souza
ILLUSTRATED BY Jennifer Wagner

TO MY DENTIST

Thank you for your authenticity,

inspiration, quality banter,

excellent dental skills,

and for lunch that one time.

Kevin Kevins is in the business of helping people.
You see, **Kevin** is a dentist. He helps his patients be
healthier and happier. And he's very good at it.

Hannah is one of **Kevin's** patients.
She visits **Kevin** and his team a lot due to
her excessive dental needs.
During one of her many appointments,
they talked about skiing and thought
it would be fun to ski together.

While away at a winter wonderland with his family,
Kevin grabbed his skis and set out for a slide
on the slopes. The snow was deep, the sky was blue,
and it was a beautiful day for some fun in the sun.

Hannah and her husband, **Jeet,**
planned to meet up with **Kevin** as they were
at the same place at the same time.
After all, they all agreed it was the best place to ski.

Hannah and **Jeet** had so much fun that morning that they forgot all about **Kevin.** When they were thirsty and ready for lunch, **Hannah** checked her phone.

"Oh no," she said. **"Kevin Kevins!** I completely forgot to message him."

"Invite him to join us for lunch," said **Jeet.**

Hey, let's meet up on the hill!

Where are you guys?

Hellllllooooo?

Kevin told **Hannah** he had already snarfed some poutine on the hill, but he met up with them anyway. They talked, laughed, and quenched their thirst as **Hannah** and **Jeet** munched on their lunch. They only mentioned teeth a couple of times.

Then **Kevin** did something that caught **Hannah** and **Jeet** by surprise. When they finished their lunch and were ready to leave, he paid the bill.

"You don't have to do that!" said **Jeet.**

"That's outrageous!" said **Hannah.**
She didn't understand as neither
of them expected **Kevin** to pay.
Against their protests, he paid anyway.

"Thank you, **Kevin Kevins!**" said **Jeet.**
"I'm so mad at you!" said **Hannah.** She meant to say
thank you, which she eventually did later on.

Kevin laughed. "I'll see you on Thursday,"
he said as he waved goodbye and left
to ski with his wonderful family.

Hannah and **Jeet** were grateful for his generosity,
but they both felt that it was unnecessary.
So, they did what any typical couple would do.

They stayed up all that night and spent all the next day planning, plotting, and scheming ways to repay **Kevin** for his good deed.

"Let's buy him an awesome t-shirt!" said **Jeet**.
"We could send a fancy plant to his dental office," said **Hannah.**

"What if we took him out

for lunch in return?"

asked **Jeet.**

"Maybe I could write a book for him!"

said **Hannah.**

They looked at each other in silence.

"Hmmm," **Hannah** eventually said.

"Perhaps that's a bit too much."

Nothing seemed to be appropriate to repay **Kevin.**

"Hold on," said **Hannah** slowly. "When we do nice things for others, what is it that we want in return?"

"Nothing," said **Jeet.** "That's not why we do nice things."

"Exactly," she said. "We don't do nice things for others to get something back. So why don't we pay it forward?"

"Pay it forward?"
asked **Jeet.**

"Yes! Pay it forward.
We do something nice for
someone else instead. Then,
they can do something nice
for someone else, and then
everyone will be doing nice
things for others."

"Ah, pay it forward!
That is perfect!" said **Jeet.**

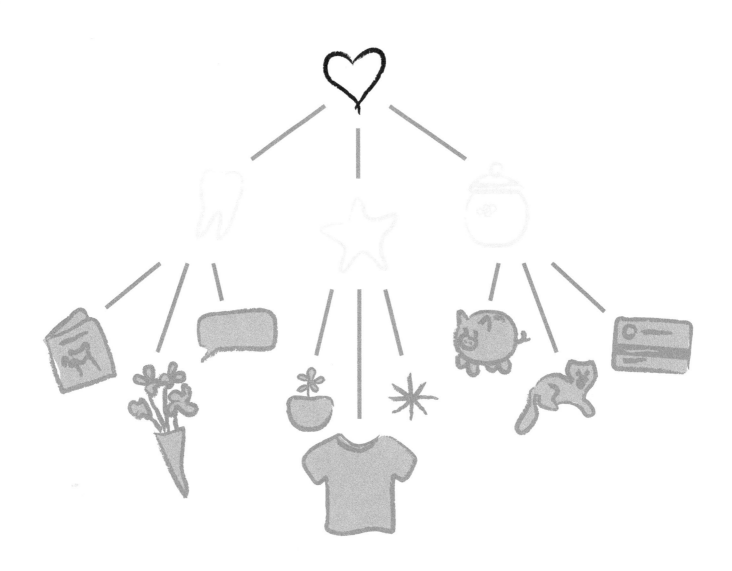

After that, their planning, plotting, and scheming changed from repaying **Kevin** for his good deed to doing good deeds for others in their community.

They volunteered, donated food and clothing, and they did their best to be kind to others. **Hannah** also made sure to recommend **Kevin** and his team to anyone who needed a good dentist.

Doing nice things for others was easy, and it felt great.

Hannah smiled.

"This is perfect," she said.

"I think I'll still write that book,

though."

AND SHE DID.

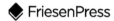

One Printers Way
Altona, MB
R0G0B0
Canada

www.friesenpress.com

Copyright © 2021 by Anna de Souza
First Edition — 2021

All rights reserved.

Illustrated by Jennifer Wagner

ISBN
978-1-03-910517-1 (Hardcover)
978-1-03-910516-4 (Paperback)
978-1-03-910518-8 (eBook)

1. *JUVENILE FICTION, SOCIAL ISSUES, MANNERS & ETIQUETTE*

Distributed to the trade by The Ingram Book Company

CPSIA information can be obtained
at www.ICGtesting.com
Printed in the USA
BVHW020800191121
622009BV00002B/45